THE LEGENDS OF KING ARTHUR

MERLIN, MAGIC AND DRAGONS

Dados Internacionais de Catalogação na Publicação (CIP) de acordo com ISBD

M469t   Mayhew, Tracey
          Tristan and Isolde / adaptado por Tracey Mayhew. – Jandira : W. Books, 2025.
          96 p. ; 12,8cm x 19,8cm. – (The legends of king Arthur)

          ISBN: 978-65-5294-167-1

          1. Literatura infantojuvenil. 2. Literatura Infantil. 3. Clássicos. 4. Literatura inglesa. 5. Lendas. 6. Folclore. 7. Mágica. 8. Cultura Popular. I. Título. II. Série

2025-616   CDD 028.5
                                                                                        CDU 82-93

Elaborado por Vagner Rodolfo da Silva - CRB-8/9410
Índice para catálogo sistemático:
1. Literatura infantojuvenil 028.5
2. Literatura infantojuvenil 82-93

The Legends of King Arthur: Merlin, Magic, and Dragons
Text © Sweet Cherry Publishing Limited, 2020
Inside illustrations © Sweet Cherry Publishing Limited, 2020
Cover illustrations © Sweet Cherry Publishing Limited, 2020

Text by Tracey Mayhew
Illustrations by Mike Phillips

© 2025 edition:
Ciranda Cultural Editora e Distribuidora Ltda.

1st edition in 2025
www.cirandacultural.com.br
No part of this publication may be reproduced, stored in a retrieval system, or transmitted in any form or by any means, electronic, mechanical, photocopying, recording, or otherwise, without written permission of the publisher.
This book is a work of fiction. Names, characters, places, and incidents are either the product of the author's imagination or are used fictitiously, and any resemblance to actual persons, living or dead, business establishments, events, or locales is entirely coincidental.

The Legends of King Arthur

TRISTAN AND ISOLDE

Retold by
Tracey Mayhew

Illustrated by
Mike Phillips

W. Books

Chapter One

Tristan de Lyonesse and his opponent charged towards each other, lances lowered and ready to strike. Tristan braced for impact, but was still rocked backwards as the other lance crashed against his shield. His own glanced off his opponent's armoured shoulder.

Splinters of wood flew and spectators cheered.

As Tristan turned his horse, he was pleased to see, through the slit of his visor, that his lance was still intact. He looked towards the other end of the arena. His opponent was adjusting to the weight of a new lance, as he exchanged a few words with Kay.

Wasting no time, Tristan spurred his horse. Looking up, his opponent sprang into action, slapping his visor back down with his shield arm and surging to meet Tristan head-on. Again they clashed, only this time Tristan's lance smashed into the red and white of Lancelot du Lac's shield, unseating him.

Reining his horse, Tristan turned hard. He was ready to charge again, but seeing Lancelot still sprawled on the ground, he knew that he had won. Tristan raised his lance in triumph, and revelled in the excited cheers as he guided his horse around the arena in a lap of victory. Returning to his end of the arena, he gave Sir Percival his lance and shield, before dismounting and handing the reins to a stable boy. He strode over to Lancelot.

'A good match,' he declared, offering his hand.

Lancelot took it. 'A good blow!' He removed his helmet and shook his head, looking slightly dazed.

At the sight of the two best jousters in Camelot shaking hands, the crowd cheered all the more joyfully. The pair waved in return, before bowing to the king and queen.

Arthur stood, raising his arms to silence the crowd. 'I declare Tristan de Lyonesse the victor!'

The Knights of the Round Table gathered in the arena to congratulate both men on a good joust. When the revelry had died down, Arthur held his hand out for Guinevere and led her back to the castle. The knights followed.

'I'll let you have this victory,' Lancelot smiled at Tristan. 'But next time, it will be you lying in the dirt whilst *I* take the victory lap!'

Before Tristan had arrived in Camelot a few years ago, no one could beat Lancelot in a joust. In the years since, it had become a

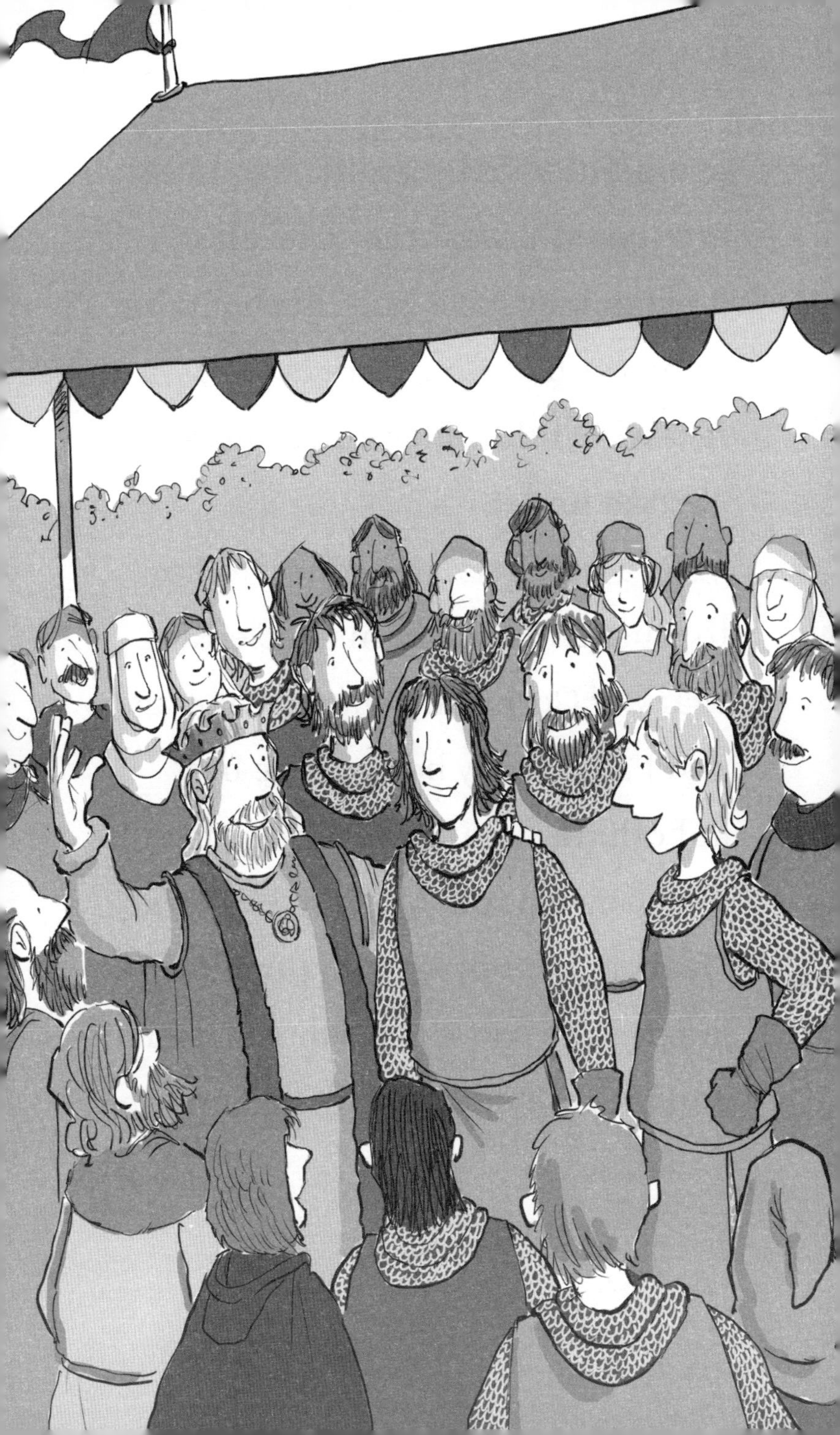

competition between the two to see who could unseat the other first. Tristan may have won this bout, but Lancelot had won more overall – a fact which the older knight never let Tristan forget.

As a boy, Tristan had learnt how to joust and hunt in his uncle King Mark of Cornwall's court at Tintagel, and had quickly become the best at both. In time, however, Tristan had grown bored of life in Cornwall. Hearing tales of King Arthur and his knights, he had travelled to Camelot and found his place at the Round Table.

'Sir Tristan!'

Tristan turned at the sound of his name to find a young squire, King Arthur's nephew, making his way towards him. 'Yes, Mordred?'

Mordred held out a scroll. 'This came for you.'

Tristan recognised his uncle's seal: a shield displaying three lion heads. Breaking the seal, he unrolled the parchment and began to read.

♦

Tristan entered Arthur's receiving room and made his way to the king. Arthur looked up from his conversation with Merlin at his approach.

'Tristan?' Arthur asked. 'Is something wrong?'

Tristan came to a stop, bowing. 'Your Majesty, I need to speak with you urgently.'

'Of course. Tell me what bothers you.'

'I have received a message from my uncle.'

Arthur looked concerned. 'Is Mark unwell?'

'He calls me back to Tintagel, Your Majesty,' Tristan explained. 'The giant Morholt, brother-in-law to King Gorlam of Ireland, has defeated my uncle's forces. As a tribute, he now demands that thirty men of noble birth be sent to him to become servants of Gorlam's court. I must return to Cornwall to help.'

'Of course,' Arthur agreed. 'I shall accompany–'

'No!' Tristan shook his head. 'Forgive me, my king, but I must return alone. Otherwise Morholt may see it as an act of war.'

Arthur sighed. 'You are right, of course. But you must promise me that you will call on me if needed.'

Tristan bowed. 'Of course, Your Majesty.'

Reaching out, Arthur placed a hand on his shoulder. 'And you must return to Camelot when this is over.'

'You have my word,' Tristan agreed.

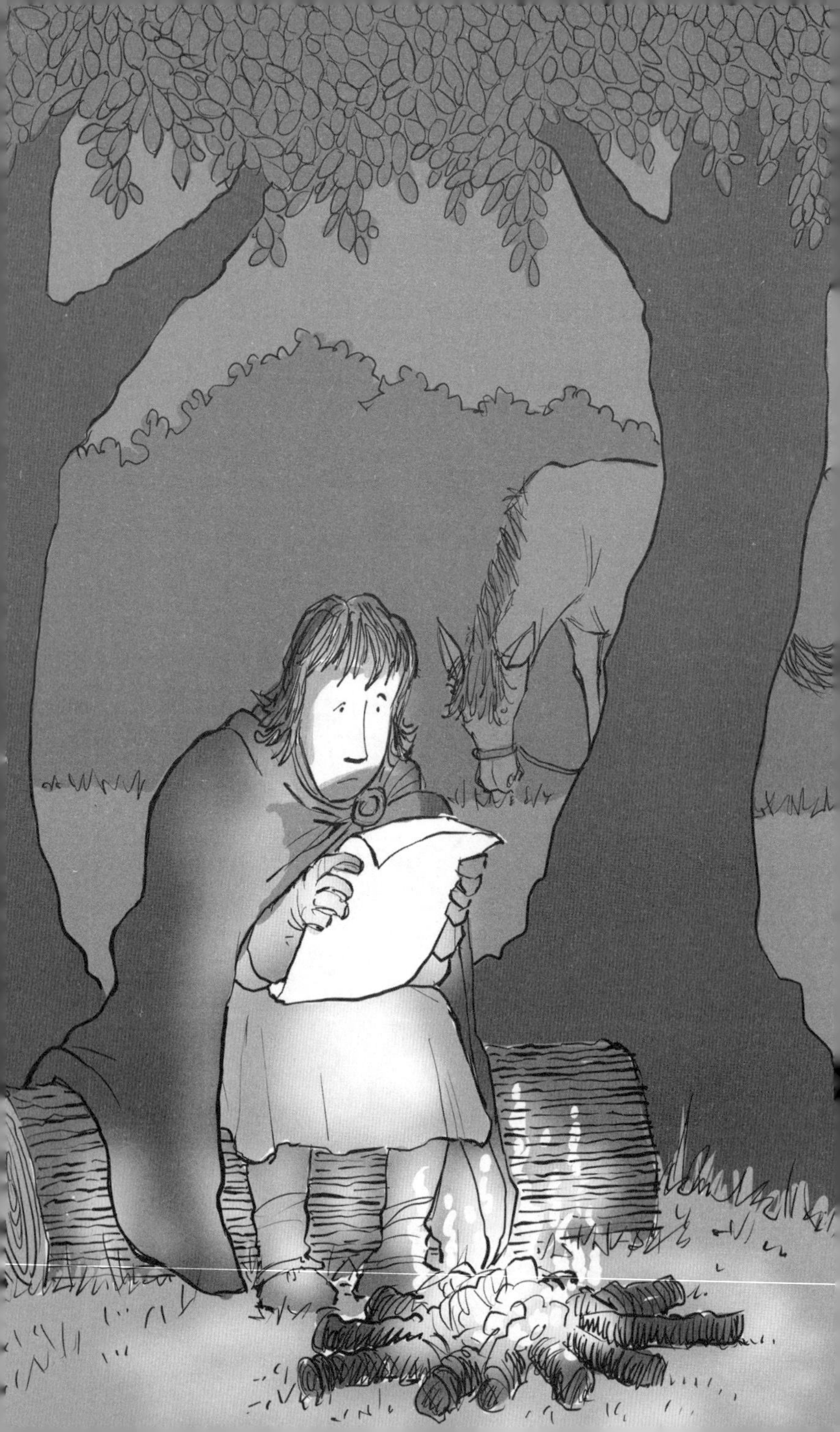

Chapter Two

Tristan rode hard to Tintagel, only stopping when darkness fell. His short nights were spent worrying about what was happening to his uncle, the man he had come to look upon as a father. By the light of the campfire, he read and reread Mark's words, hoping that he would arrive before his uncle was persuaded by his advisors to give in to Morholt's demands.

Finally arriving at Tintagel, Tristan found Morholt's men camped outside.

Slowing his horse, Tristan made his way towards the gatehouse, watching each man carefully as he passed, alert for any sign of attack.

Tristan reined his horse to a stop as a giant stepped into his path. Although wearing armour, the giant had no helmet and a ragged scar ran down his left cheek.

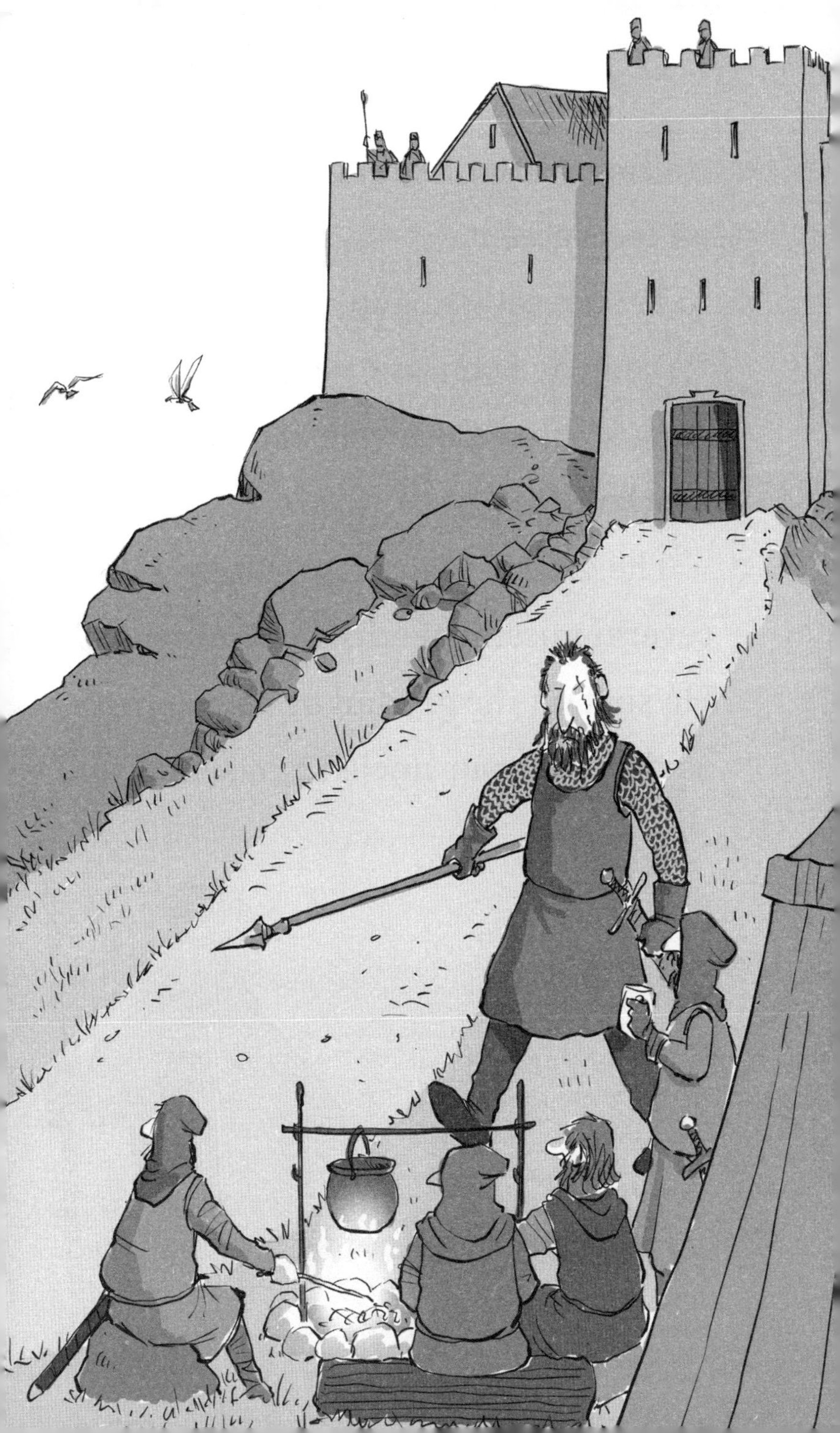

'Your name?' the giant demanded in an Irish accent.

Tristan sat straighter in his saddle. 'Tristan de Lyonesse, nephew of King Mark of Cornwall. You must be Morholt.'

The giant grinned, revealing several missing teeth. '*Duke* Morholt.' He spat on the ground as he stepped aside. 'Tell your uncle he has until sundown to give me what I came for, or send out a man brave enough to fight me.'

Tristan held Morholt's gaze for a moment before snapping his reins and continuing on.

♣

'But, uncle, we cannot give in!' Tristan insisted.

Mark sighed. 'We just don't see any other way, Tristan.'

'So you would all rather have your sons sent to live as servants in Ireland than stand up to Morholt?' Tristan asked in disbelief, looking around at Mark and his advisors.

'Have you seen him?' one of his uncle's advisors squeaked.

'Then *I* will challenge him,' Tristan declared, storming from the room.

Mark hurried after him. 'Are you sure about this, Tristan? Your bravery is well known but Morholt is a monster!'

'I am not afraid, uncle.'

They were soon at the gatehouse, where Morholt was waiting.

'Has the cowardly king finally made

a decision?' he mocked.

'I will fight you,' Tristan said, loudly enough for all to hear.

It was decided that the duel would take place on a small island not far off the coast of Cornwall. Two boats were made ready, one for Tristan, the other for Morholt. The following day, they both rowed out to the island.

'Only one of us will leave here,' Morholt declared, pushing his boat back out to sea, so that only Tristan's remained on the beach. 'This will only end when one of us is dead.'

'As you wish,' Tristan agreed as he raised his shield.

The two men circled, sizing each other up. Tristan made the first move, his sword flashing in the sun, but Morholt's spear easily pushed it aside.

Spinning the butt of his spear around, Morholt tried to sweep Tristan's legs out from under him. Tristan dodged and countered with a blow that caught Morholt's arm, drawing blood.

Roaring with rage, Morholt thrust his spear forward, piercing Tristan's thigh. Tristan fell to the ground, crying out as Morholt pulled his spear from the wound. Blood soaked his trousers, but Tristan climbed clumsily to his feet, gritting his teeth against the pain shooting through his leg.

Morholt laughed. 'I admire you, Tristan de Lyonesse, but your bravery is no good to you now. My spear point is poisoned.' The giant bent his head to gloat. 'You are dead already, although it will not come quickly.'

'Coward!' Tristan roared. His pain exploded into rage as he launched himself at Morholt, driving his sword through his skull. Morholt eyes flew wide with shock, and stayed that way as he dropped lifelessly to the ground.

Tristan pulled his sword from the giant's head. Turning, he limped towards his boat and threw his sword and shield into it. It took almost all his remaining strength to push the boat out to sea and heave himself aboard. Picking up the oars, he used the rest to row away from the shore, hoping that he could make it back to Tintagel alive.

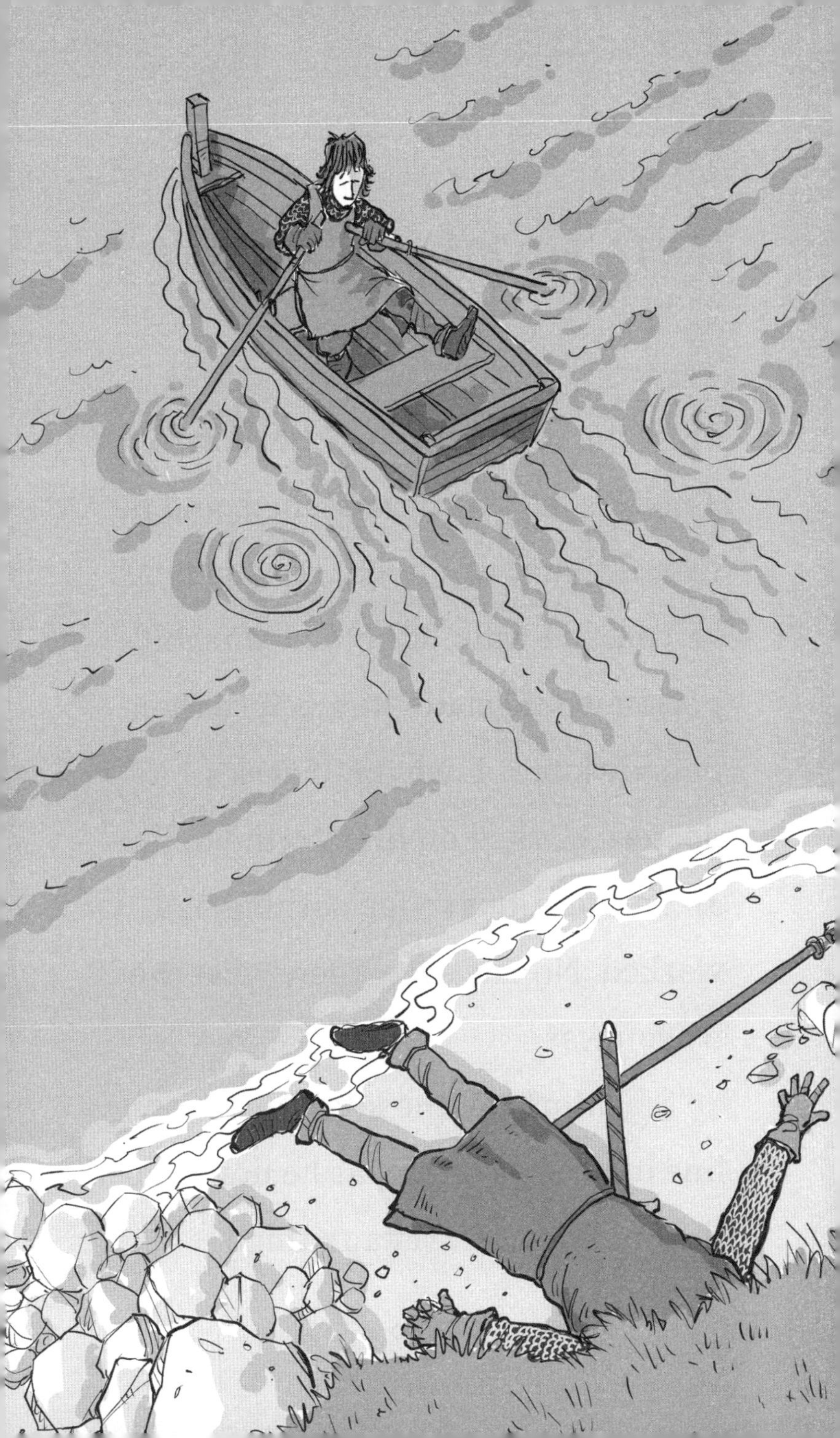

Chapter Three

Over the next few days, the pain in Tristan's leg slowly worsened, and he feared that it would not be long until he couldn't walk. Whether Morholt's poison would claim him before then, nobody knew. Each day, Mark's doctors worked on him, trying to find an antidote, but so far nothing had worked. No one even knew what the poison was.

'Sir,' Morfran, the latest in a long line of doctors began, as he unwrapped the bindings on Tristan's thigh, 'have you considered that the antidote may be in Ireland?'

'Ireland?' Mark echoed. He had not left Tristan's side since his return.

As the last of the bindings fell away, the smell of rotting flesh filled the room. The three men recoiled and, holding their noses, gazed at the wound. It looked no worse than before, but the smell coming from it was enough to turn their stomachs.

As Morfran applied a fresh poultice, he said, 'I have heard that King Gorlam's wife, Queen Isolde the Elder, has great knowledge of plants and herbs. If this poison comes from Ireland, then so may the antidote.'

'*May?*' Mark echoed again. 'You don't sound very sure.'

'It is better than doing nothing, uncle!' Tristan cried. 'And we've tried everything else. I shall go to Ireland.'

Mark scoffed. 'And get yourself killed? Have you forgotten that Morholt was King Gorlam's brother-in-law?'

Tristan glanced at his sword, the tip of which was now gone, lost in Morholt's wound. 'If I don't go, I will just as surely die *here*.' He paused. 'Besides, I can go in disguise.'

Mark looked doubtful, but Tristan quickly warmed to his plan.

'I could go as a travelling minstrel, wounded on my journey.'

'It could work,' Mark admitted reluctantly. 'But I won't have you travelling alone. Morfran will go with you, in case your condition worsens.'

'As you wish, Your Majesty,' Morfran agreed, tying fresh bindings around Tristan's thigh.

The following day, Tristan set sail for Ireland disguised as Tantris, a travelling harpist. The crossing was long and the rough sea sent waves crashing onto the deck. Tristan spent much of his time in his cabin below, his leg throbbing.

Eventually, they reached the shores of Ireland. Tristan and Morfran travelled by donkey and cart to King

Gorlam's castle, where they were greeted by the king and queen.

'Your Majesties,' Tristan said, bowing as low as his injured leg allowed, 'my name is Tantris and I have come to your court to entertain you with the finest music!'

King Gorlam looked down at him from his throne. 'The finest music, you say? Even better than the musicians of my court? Prove it!'

Tristan bowed again before sitting with his harp. The guests in the hall fell silent as Tristan plucked a few strings, tuning the harp. When he began to play, he closed his eyes, losing himself to the music as the notes rose and fell.

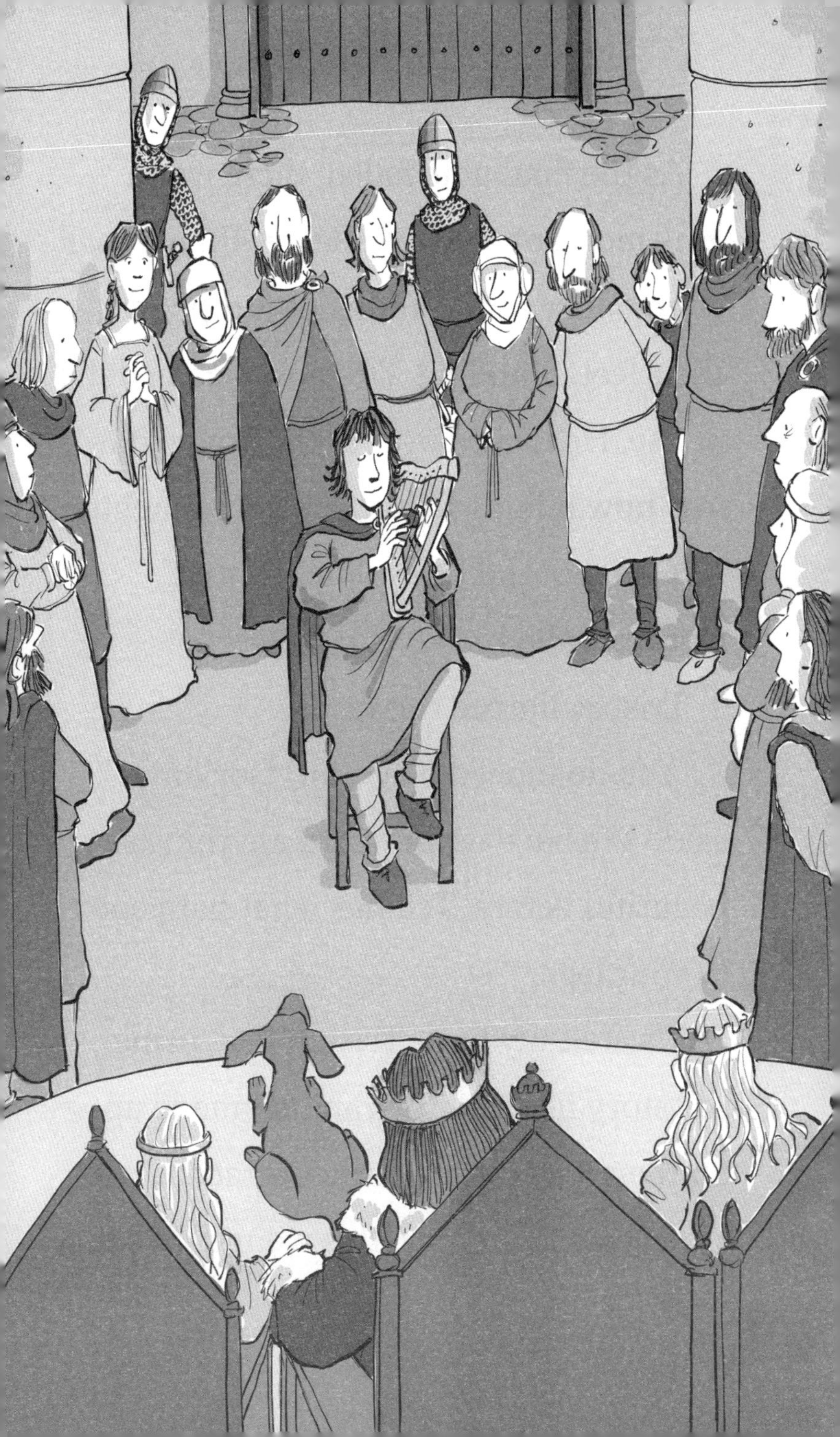

As the final note faded, there was a long moment of awed silence, then a roar of applause as the audience jumped to their feet. Standing, Tristan welcomed the praise. He looked over at the king who was now talking to his wife and daughter.

'Come, stand before me, Tantris,' Gorlam called.

Tristan limped forwards.

'You do indeed play well,' Gorlam said. 'We have never heard anything so beautiful before. Tell me, what happened to your leg?'

'Pirates, my lord,' Tristan lied, using the story he and Morfran had made up on their way there. 'Pirates attacked our ship, leaving me with this wound.'

The king nodded. 'My wife, Queen Isolde, says she can heal you. But there is a condition.'

'Name it, Your Majesty.'

'You must teach our daughter how to play the harp.'

Tristan glanced at Isolde the Fair, who was as beautiful as her name suggested, and bowed. 'As you wish, Your Majesty.'

And so it was that Tristan spent the next forty days in King Gorlam's court, teaching the fair Isolde how to play the harp. Day by day, his leg grew stronger, thanks to the concoctions Queen Isolde the Elder made for him.

The time spent with the princess was time Tristan treasured, and they grew to be great friends. But when Tristan's leg was fully healed, the time had come for him to leave and return to Cornwall.

'I will miss you, Tantris,' Isolde murmured sadly.

'I will miss you, too,' Tristan said.

'Perhaps one day you will return to Ireland.'

'Perhaps,' he agreed. 'If I do, you can play for me.'

The princess smiled hopefully, and Tristan immediately felt guilty. He knew that he would never return to Ireland, nor hear Isolde play the harp again.

He was wrong on both counts.

Chapter Four

'And she truly is as beautiful as you say?' Mark asked for perhaps the hundredth time.

Tristan smiled at his uncle. Ever since the day Tristan had arrived back in Cornwall, Mark had wanted to hear tales of Isolde the Fair's beauty and charms. Tristan had never seen him so infatuated.

'I wonder if I might make her my wife,' Mark mused, looking around at his advisors.

'Impossible,' Tristan argued.

'Don't forget, the Irish hate us for killing Morholt.'

'But King Gorlam has no male heir. If I take his daughter as my wife, we could make peace and unite our kingdoms.'

'That is true, Your Majesty,' Godwin, one of Mark's advisors, said. 'Peace between Ireland and Cornwall would be a great thing.'

'Indeed it would,' Ganelon, another advisor, agreed.

Tristan shook his head. 'The Irish seek revenge not unity!'

Ganelon shook his head. 'Not necessarily. I have heard tales from merchants about a dragon terrorising Ireland. According to them, the king and queen have promised their daughter's hand to anyone brave enough to slay it.'

Mark grinned. 'Well, then this is my chance! I shall go–'

'No, uncle,' Tristan protested. 'You must stay here. I have been to Ireland already – I know the land and its people. I will slay the dragon and win Isolde's hand for you.'

'You would do that?'

Tristan bowed his head. 'I would.'

Later that day, Tristan set sail back to Ireland. Once there, fully armed and wearing his knight's armour instead of his minstrel's clothes, he set out in search of the dragon.

It didn't take him long to find a path of destruction. The charred remains of villages and farmlands led the way to the foot of a mountain. Climbing the steep path, Tristan found himself at the mouth of a cave, where he paused cautiously and strained his ears …

That was when he heard it: a roar, deep within the mountain.

Readying his spear and shield, Tristan stepped up to the cave. He hesitated outside, reluctant to exchange the bright blue daylight for blackest night. Desperate cries came from the darkness, and Tristan almost struck the man who came sprinting suddenly out of it. His sooty face was a mask of fear, the whites of his eyes almost glowing within it. The man barely spared Tristan or his spear a glance as he shot from the cave and down the mountainside. A thin trail of smoke drifted after him, staining the otherwise clear sky. Heat followed. Heat so intense it drove Tristan back several steps, ducking behind the cover of his shield. His armour warmed unbearably.

A dragon lumbered into sight, stealing what breath Tristan had left. It towered over him, blue-green scales shining as it stretched translucent wings. Its tail flicked almost lazily towards Tristan, who threw himself to the ground just in time to avoid it.

Finding his feet, Tristan thrust his spear at the dragon's back legs. The dragon roared and slashed its tail again – not lazy now. Tristan deflected it with his shield, but was sent sprawling to the ground. Crawling over to the nearest rock, he watched as the dragon looked

to the sky and roared, releasing an enormous jet of fire. Turning its head, the dragon's eyes found Tristan and shot another stream of fire straight at him.

Tristan ducked, covering his head with his shield and letting the rock take the rest of the dragon's fire. As the flames died, Tristan raced out from behind the rock, ducked between the dragon's forelegs, raised his spear, and pierced the dragon's belly.

The dragon roared and launched itself into the sky, only to double back, diving straight at Tristan with its mouth gaping wide. Tristan had a glimpse of a forked red tongue and needle-like teeth before he dived out of the way. Pain shot through his body as he rolled along the mountainside.

His head hit a boulder and he saw stars. He needed to end this soon, before he was too tired or injured to have any hope of winning. Before the dragon flew out of reach.

As the dragon dove towards him once more, Tristan met it head-on. With a cry that made his throat raw, Tristan thrust his spear before the dragon could release another burst of fire that would surely kill him. The spear ripped through the creature's neck, sending it crashing back down to the mountain.

Tristan drew his sword and approached the body. He stood over it for a moment, before nudging it with his toe once, twice.

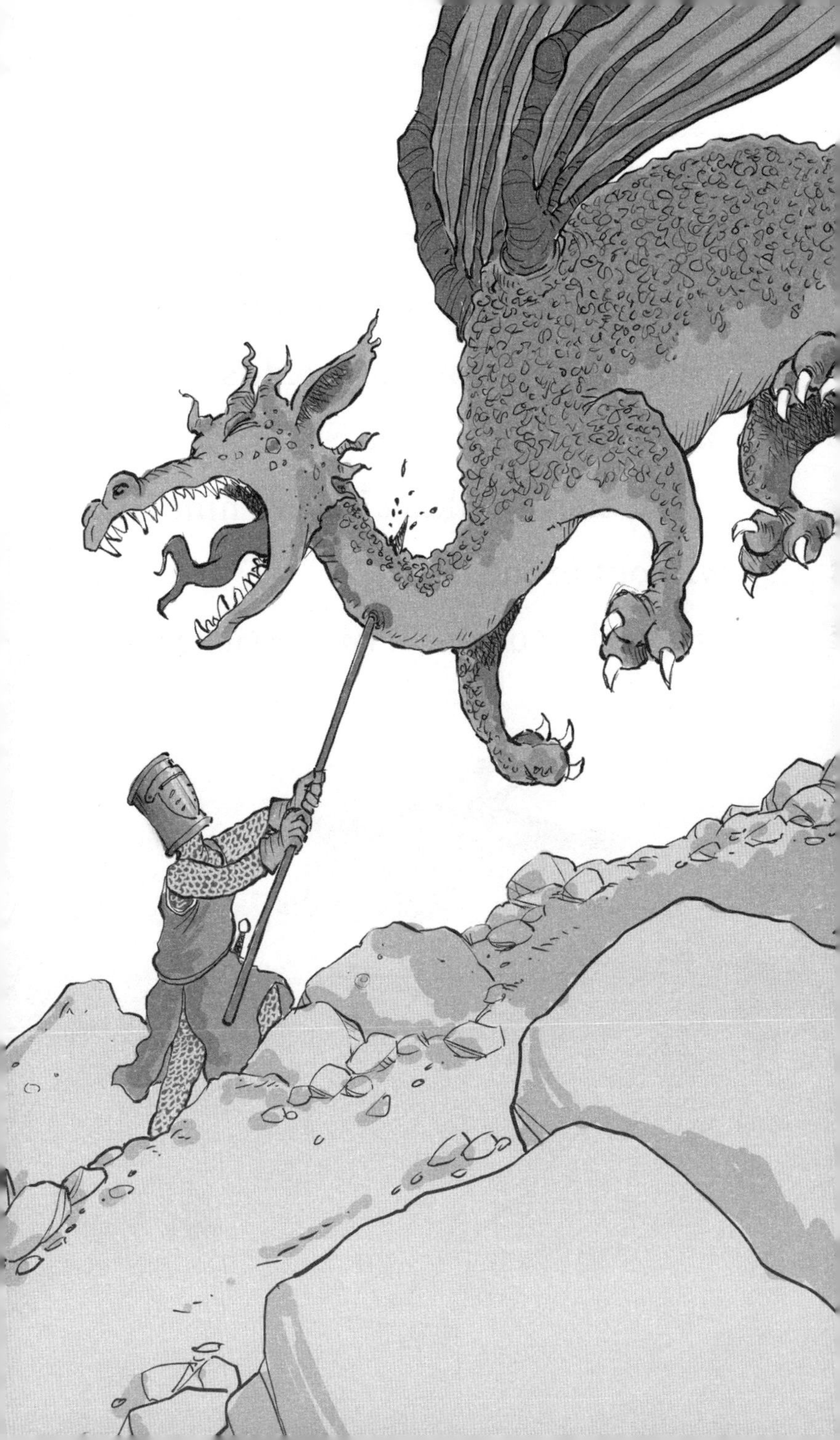

It was dead.

Tristan had killed the dragon. He could go to King Gorlam and declare himself the winner of Isolde's hand, on behalf of his uncle.

But they wouldn't believe him without proof.

Kneeling down, Tristan reached for

the tongue lolling from the dragon's mouth. With one stroke of his sword, he cut it off and set out for King Gorlam's court. However, with each step he took, Tristan began to grow weaker and weaker, until he could barely stand. Darkness crept at the edge of his vision. Then he fell to his knees, and knew no more.

Chapter Five

King Gorlam stared at the tall, pale figure of his steward. The armour he wore was battered, the sword at his side bloodstained, his face almost black with soot. When he had set out to kill the dragon a few days ago, no one had believed he would make it back alive, let alone successful.

But the dragon head at his feet told a different tale.

'You're telling me it was *you* who killed this beast?' the king wanted to confirm.

His steward stood tall. 'Yes, Your Majesty. I killed the beast and cut off its head as proof.'

Isolde held her breath. Surely her father would see through the steward's lies. There was no way such a coward could have done this.

'Very well, then,' Gorlam sighed. 'Isolde's hand is yours.'

Hearing these words, Isolde glared at her father, before standing up and marching from the room. There was no way she would marry that man!

'Isolde!'

The sound of her mother's voice stopped Isolde in her tracks. She clenched her skirts in tight fists. 'Mother, I refuse to marry him! I don't care what father says, I will–!'

'Hush, my child,' her mother soothed. 'I do not believe he killed the dragon.'

'You don't?' Isolde asked hopefully.

Her mother shook her head. 'No. But we must find proof.'

'How do we do that?'

The queen smiled. 'We must find the man who *did* kill the dragon.'

Leaving the castle with a manservant to accompany them, Isolde and her mother tracked the path the steward had described in his heroic tale. It wasn't long before they came across a knight lying just off the path, hidden in the undergrowth.

The queen ordered the manservant to return to the castle and fetch help. Then she and her daughter knelt and turned the man over.

'It's Tantris!' Isolde cried.

The queen still studied the man's face. 'Are you sure?'

'I am certain of it.' Isolde's eyes drifted to Tristan's hand. 'What is that he carries?'

The queen grabbed her wrist as Isolde reached out. 'Don't touch it!' she hissed. 'I fear this is the reason Tantris has fallen ill.'

'What do you mean? What is it?'

'I think we have found our dragon-slayer,' the queen murmured, as she wrapped the strange object in linen. Reaching into a pouch on her belt, she pulled out a bottle of clear liquid and put it to Tantris's lips. A few drops fell into his mouth. 'This should give him enough strength to make it back to the castle where I can help him further.'

Tantris's eyes began to open.

'Tantris!' Isolde cried.

'Princess,' he croaked.

The manservant returned with another man, carrying a litter between them. Lifting Tantris onto it, they set off back to the castle.

It wasn't until the next day that Tantris was well enough to speak, and the true story of how the dragon had been slain was revealed.

King Gorlam stared at him. 'How do I know you speak the truth?'

'I cut out the dragon's tongue.'

Beside Tantris, the steward scoffed. 'You would believe this *liar* over me, my lord?'

'It is true, husband,' Queen Isolde confirmed, ignoring the steward's outburst. 'He was still clutching it when we found him. It was poisonous.'

'Let me see,' said the king.

At the queen's signal the doors opened, and two manservants came in carrying the dragon's head on a litter. They placed it before the king. The mouth had been opened and the tongue placed back in its rightful place.

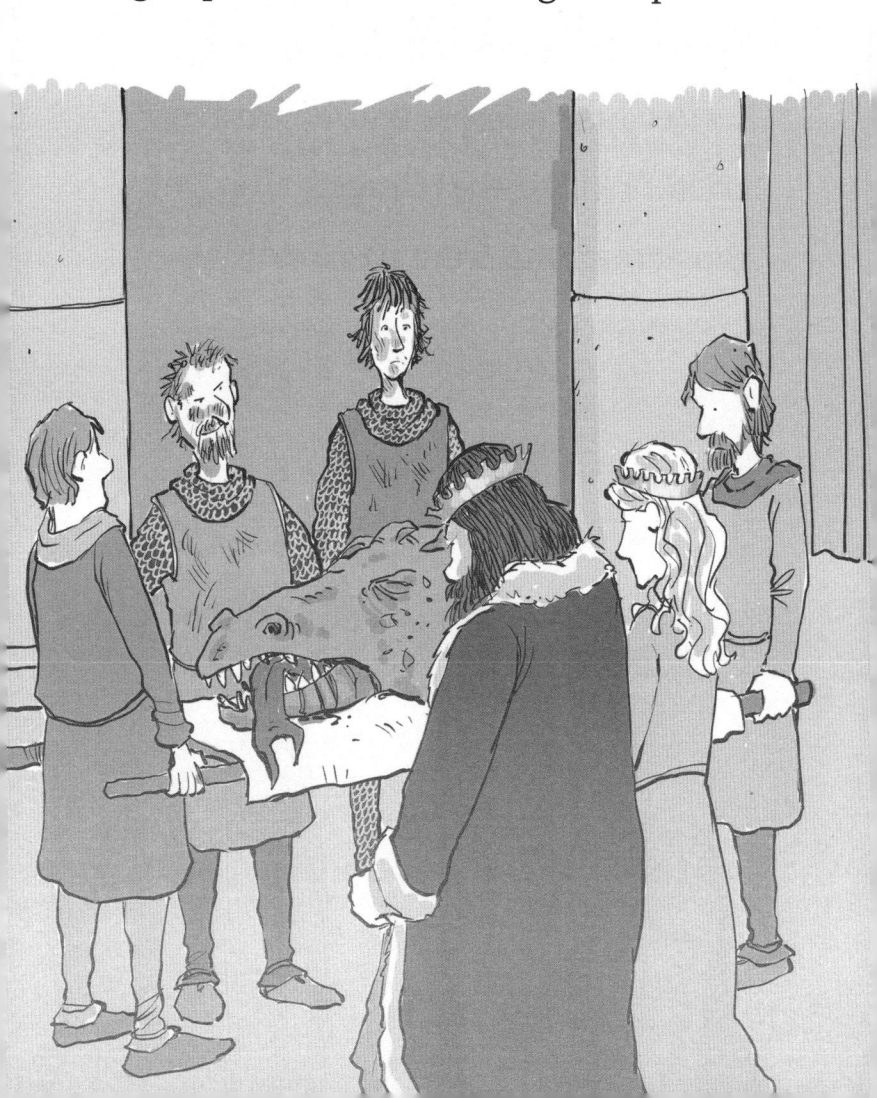

Gorlam looked up at his steward. 'You lied to your king.'

'I have served you loyally!' the steward protested desperately. 'How can you believe this – this musician over me?'

'Because it is the truth!' Tantris cried. 'I killed that dragon after you ran screaming from its cave.'

'Then I challenge you to a duel!' the steward declared. 'Let us see who is the braver man!'

'Very well,' Tantris agreed.

The next day, Isolde went to find Tantris in order to wish him luck. She found him sharpening his sword in the courtyard, but stopped as her eyes caught sight of the blade.

The tip was missing.

Could this be the sword tip they had found inside the wound that killed her uncle?

Opening the pouch at her waist, Isolde pulled a small piece of iron from it. She had kept it since her uncle's death, when his body was returned to them by their enemies across the sea.

Taking a step towards the broken sword, Isolde reached out …

To her dismay, the piece fitted perfectly.

Chapter Six

'Father! Mother!' Isolde cried as she entered the queen's sitting room, two guards dragging Tristan behind her. 'I bring terrible news! The man we know as Tantris, harp player and dragon slayer, is also the man who murdered your brother!'

'Is this true?' the queen asked Tristan shakily.

'It is, Your Majesty,' he admitted. 'But I was defending my home and my people.'

'Then why did you come to Ireland? To see the pain you had caused?'

Tristan shook his head. 'The wound I had when I first arrived was the result of Morholt's poisoned spear, which only you could cure. And

I am here now to win Isolde's hand for King Mark, my uncle, who wants peace between our two kingdoms.'

Hearing this, Isolde scoffed. But King Gorlam, reacting for the first time, signalled for the guards to release Tristan. 'And your real name is?'

'Sir Tristan de Lyonesse, Your Majesty.'

'And you say your uncle wishes peace?'

'He does indeed.'

'Then perhaps we should consider it,' Gorlam declared. He silenced his wife's protest with a look. 'If you win this duel with my steward, then King Mark of

Cornwall may marry my daughter.'

'What?' Isolde cried furiously. 'You would have me marry a man who had a hand in my uncle's death? For I doubt very much that Tant– *Tristan* was acting alone.'

'King Mark is a good match for you,' Gorlam said.

'But I have no wish to marry him!'

'Then pray my steward wins.'

But when the two men met in the arena later that day, Tristan beat the steward easily. After saying a tearful farewell to her parents, Isolde boarded the boat that would take her to her new life in Cornwall. She went immediately to her cabin where she vowed to remain for the entire journey. Her maidservant, Brangwain, started to follow. She was stopped by Queen Isolde the Elder who took her to one side so that they could speak privately.

'I have something to give you,' the queen whispered, taking a bottle from beneath her cloak. 'Make sure that on their wedding day, Isolde and King Mark both drink this.'

'What is it, Your Majesty?' Brangwain asked as she took the bottle.

'It's a love potion so strong that once a man and woman have drunk it together, nothing will undo its effects. They will love each other until the end of time and beyond.'

Taking the potion, Brangwain boarded the ship and found the cabin she and Isolde would be sharing. She placed the bottle in her chest and thought nothing more of it.

The journey was rough and Brangwain soon took to her bed with seasickness. As promised, Isolde kept to the cabin at first, but soon grew bored and restless. Rummaging through the chests for something warm to wear on deck, she found a cloak and the bottle in Brangwain's luggage. Taking both, she crept up to the deck, glad to see there was no sign of Tristan.

Looking out to sea, she opened the bottle.

'It is good to see you out of your cabin at last.'

Isolde turned at the sound of Tristan's voice, but said nothing.

Tristan came to stand beside her, his eyes landing on the bottle in her grasp. 'Ah, you've brought wine, I see.' He smiled.

Automatically, despite her anger, Isolde held it out to him. 'Would you like some?'

'After you.'

Raising the bottle to her lips, Isolde drank, gasping at the bitter flavour. It didn't taste like any wine that she had ever had, but she offered it to Tristan nonetheless. Taking the bottle, Tristan drank the rest.

Swallowing his last mouthful, Tristan was vaguely aware of the bottle falling from his grasp and smashing on the deck. The rest of him was entirely focused on Isolde.

She really was the loveliest creature he had ever laid eyes upon. The world around him seemed to dim in the face of her beauty and his heart beat faster just from looking at her! Reaching out, Tristan pulled her into his arms. 'Isolde the Fairest,' he whispered as he kissed her cheek.

For many hours they stayed in each other's arms, talking only to each other and heedless of anything or anyone else. They played chess and took turns on Tristan's harp. As they sailed closer to Tintagel, they began to feel a deep sadness. Although they loved each other passionately, Isolde had been sworn to King Mark, and he was soon to be her husband.

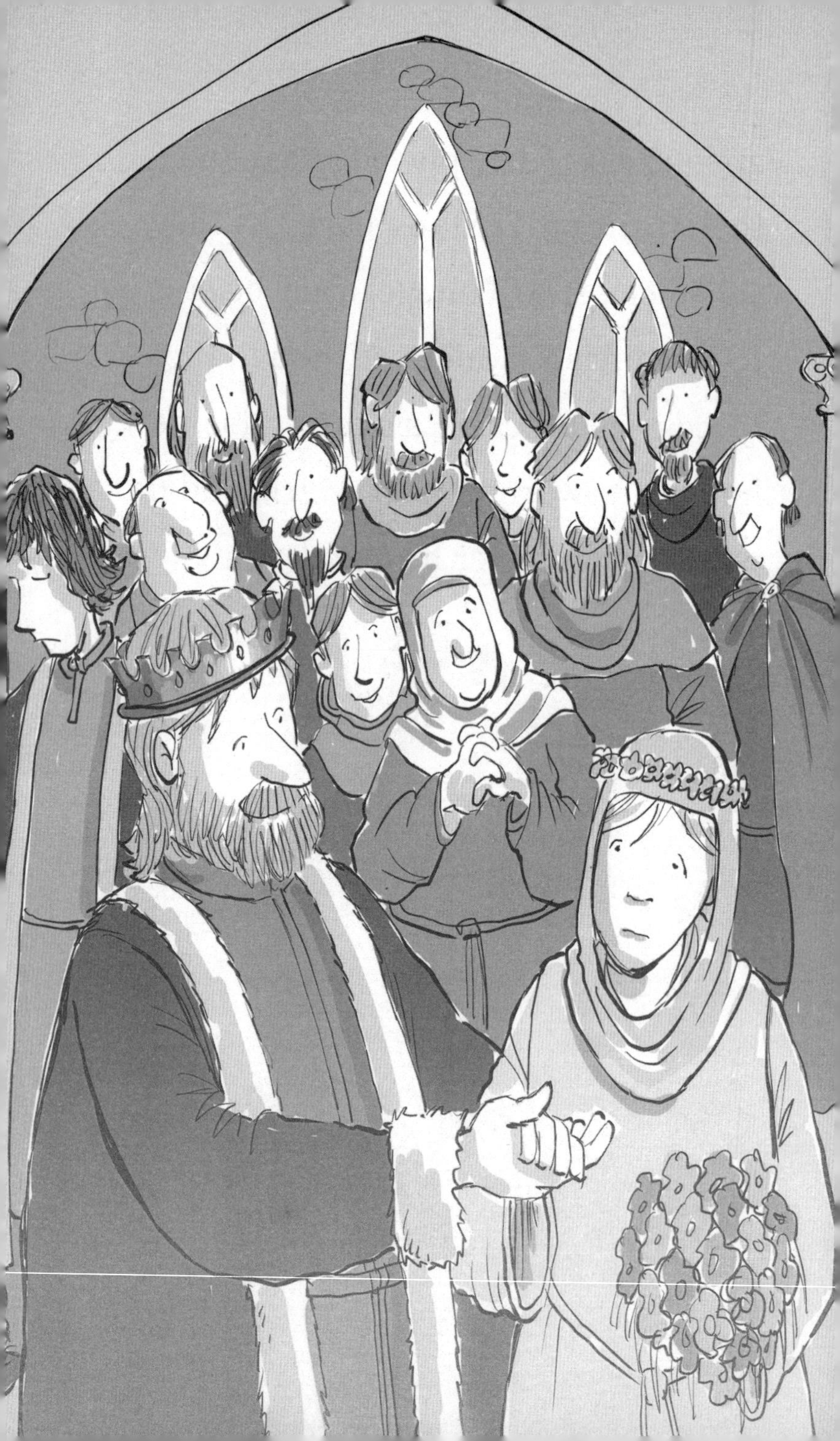

Chapter Seven

Tristan watched in agony as Isolde spoke her wedding vows to his uncle. He saw the tears in her eyes and knew that she was as heartbroken as he. He would have given anything to marry her himself, but knew that it was impossible.

Weeks turned to months and Tristan's feelings for Isolde did not weaken. He knew he should leave Tintagel and return to Camelot as he had promised King Arthur, but he could not bear the thought of so much distance separating them.

So Tristan stayed at King Mark's court, and each day grew more torturous. He could only watch Isolde from a distance, never trusting himself to be too close to her for fear that he might say or do something they would regret.

Then, one day, as he was riding through the woods, Tristan caught sight of a hooded figure on the path ahead of him.

Isolde!

Tristan's heart leapt at the sight of her. He reined his horse to a stop, barely able to contain his excitement. 'Your Majesty, what are you doing out here?'

'I had to see you,' she whispered, slipping her hands into his. 'I have missed you so.'

'I've missed you too,' he said, kissing her hands, pulling her close. Looking into each other's eyes, each felt the world stop. Nothing existed in that moment except them. Tristan leant in to kiss her …

'Traitors!'

Drawing his sword as he swung towards the enraged voice, Tristan found himself facing Mark.

'You betrayed me, nephew! Godwin suspected as much but I wouldn't believe him. Now I find you here together!' He lunged and his sword flashed.

Tristan easily deflected the attack, moving himself and Isolde backwards, out of Mark's reach. 'I am truly sorry, uncle, but I cannot help loving her!'

'You ungrateful wretch!' Mark moved to attack again. 'After all I have done for you!'

Tristan deflected each blow, never once attempting to land his own. 'I won't fight you, uncle,' he insisted.

'Then you are a coward as well as a traitor! Fight me!'

'Please!' Isolde cried, tears streaming down her face. 'There must be some other way!'

Mark looked between them, pain and anger in his eyes. Eventually, he let his sword drop to his side. 'I never thought I would see this day. My heart is broken.' Meeting Tristan's gaze, he said, 'Leave Tintagel now and never come back.

If you do, you will be executed for treason.'

The last thing Tristan wanted was to leave Tintagel. With Isolde there, it was more his home than ever. But what other choice did he have?

Taking Isolde's hands, Tristan whispered words of love and farewell, all the while ignoring her pleas to take her with him. Then he mounted his horse and rode back into the woods. Isolde's voice rang out behind him and he pressed his horse harder, desperately trying to outrun it.

Knowing that he was no longer worthy to sit at the Round Table, Tristan left Britain entirely. He sought a new home on the shores of Brittany. There he married in an attempt to forget Isolde. His new wife tried everything she could to win Tristan's heart, but it soon became clear that it belonged to another, and her heart grew bitter because of it.

One day, whilst Tristan and his friend, Kurwenal, were out hunting, Tristan was struck in the shoulder by a poisoned spear. Back home, his wife cleaned the wound, but it continued to fester until the pain was unbearable.

'You must go to Cornwall,' Tristan begged Kurwenal. 'Find Isolde the Fair and bring her here. She has surely inherited her mother's healing skills. She will help me.'

Nodding, Kurwenal left, promising to do all that he could to bring Isolde back with him.

Tristan fell into a fever. His wife spent each day caring for him and doing her best to ease his pains, even as he spoke of his true love in his sleep. On the fourth day, she caught sight of a ship on the horizon.

'What colour are the sails?' Tristan asked from his bed.

'It is too far away,' his wife replied. 'Why does it matter?'

'If they are white, then Isolde is aboard. If they are black, then she isn't coming.'

Turning back to the window, his wife looked again. Eventually she saw the white sails of the ship growing larger as it approached. Her heart sank. 'They are black,' she lied. Shaking her head, she turned to her husband. 'I'm sorry, Tristan. She isn't coming.'

Tears filled Tristan's eyes as he felt his heart break, knowing that he would never look upon Isolde's beautiful face again. Turning away, he faced the wall and drew his last breath.

His wife was still crying silently when Kurwenal arrived with a beautiful woman, and hurried into the house. Seeing Tristan's lifeless body, Isolde fell to her knees beside him. Taking his hands in hers, she sobbed passionately and did not stop. It wasn't long before she, too, died of a broken heart.

Touched by their love, Tristan's wife regretted the jealousy that had led her to lie, and wanted to make amends for her selfishness. She buried her husband next to his true love, Isolde the Fair, to be united in death, as they could not be in life. And there they rest together, until the end of time, and beyond.

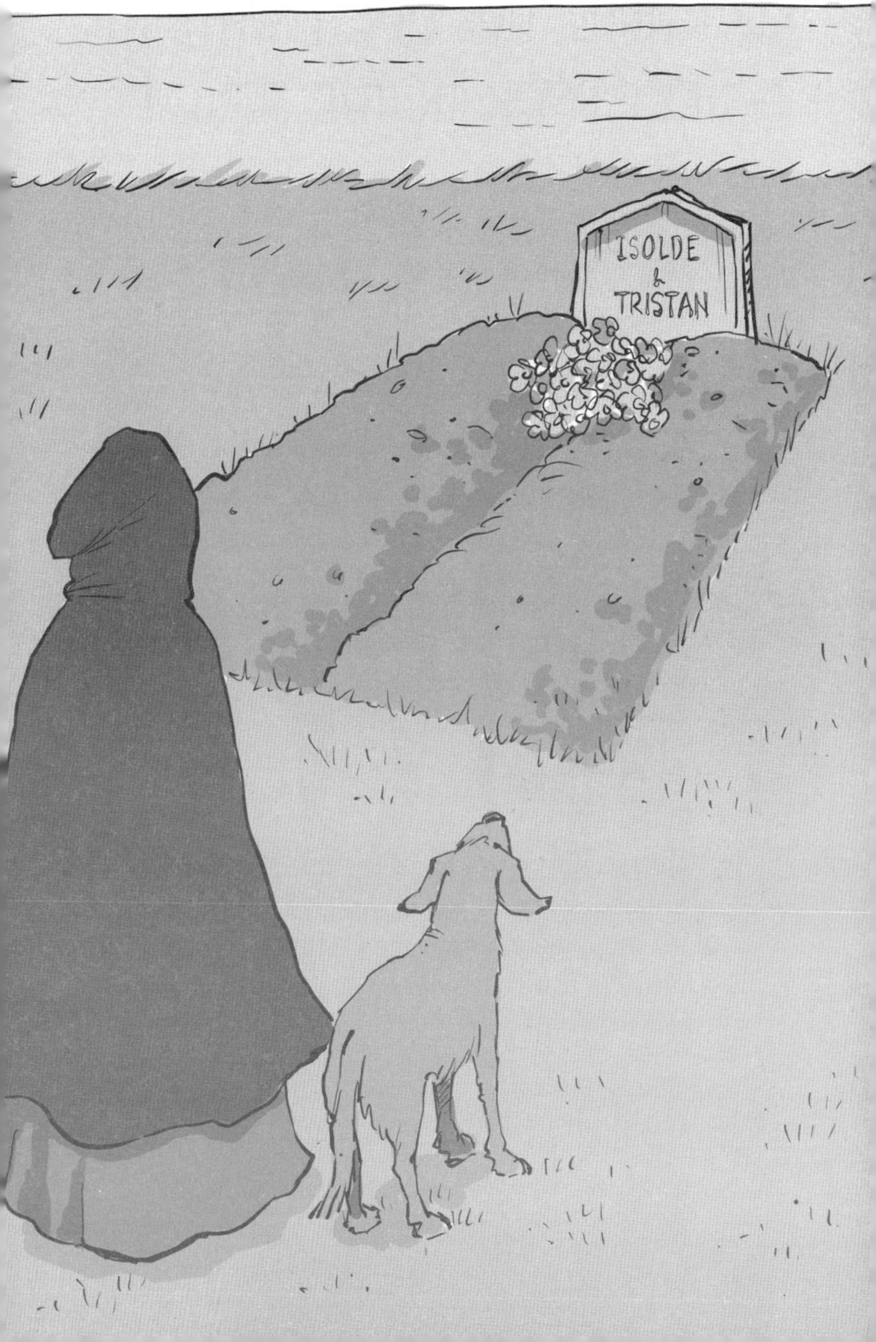
ISOLDE
&
TRISTAN

Continue the quest with the next book in the series!

The Legends of King Arthur
Lancelot
illustrated by Mike Phillips

includes FREE AUDIOBOOK!

EASY CLASSICS

"This series opens the door to a treasure house of wonderful stories which have previously been available chiefly to older readers. We can only welcome it as a fabulous resource for all who love magical tales, and those who will come to love them."

John Matthews
Author of the Red Dragon Rising series and Arthur of Albion